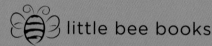 little bee books

251 Park Avenue South, New York, NY 10010
Text copyright © 2020 by Ann Bausum
Illustrations copyright © 2020 by Kyung Eun Han
All rights reserved, including the right of reproduction in whole or in part in any form.
Manufactured in China LEO 0620
For more information about special discounts on bulk purchases,
please contact Little Bee Books at sales@littlebeebooks.com.
First Edition
1 2 3 4 5 6 7 8 9 10
Library of Congress Cataloging-in-Publication Data
Names: Bausum, Ann, author. | Han, Kyung Eun, illustrator.
Title: Moonbeams / Ann Bausum; [illustrated by] Kyung Eun Han.
Description: First edition. | New York, NY: Little Bee Books, [2020]
Audience: 004–008. | Audience: K–1. | Summary: "I see the moon. Can the
moon see me? Tell me, shadow moon, what do you see? Toward the sun, I
shine quite bright, but down on Earth, there's darkest night. My first
face is fresh and new. You'll see each phase before we're through. In
this sweet bedtime story is a universal truth—we are all connected by
the moon. From Yosemite to the Taj Mahal to the coast of Greece, we all
gaze upon the same moon. Told in dual perspectives from the phases of
the moon and from people around the world, they work together to strike
a balance of humility and wonder while teaching young readers all about
the journey of the moon. Paired with gorgeous illustrations, the
rhythmic cadence of the text will lull young readers to sleep on a
whimsical, yet factual, journey!"—Provided by publisher.
Identifiers: LCCN 2019033959 | Subjects: LCSH: Moon—Juvenile
literature. | Moon—Phases—Juvenile literature.
Classification: LCC QB582.B38 2020 | DDC 523.3—dc23
LC record available at https://lccn.loc.gov/2019033959
ISBN 978-1-4998-1033-2
littlebeebooks.com

MOONBEAMS

A LULLABY OF THE PHASES OF THE MOON

words by **ANN BAUSUM**   pictures by **KYUNG EUN HAN**

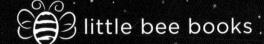
little bee books

I see the moon. Can the moon see me?
Tell me, shadow moon, what do you see?

Toward the sun, I shine quite bright,
but down on Earth, there's darkest night.
My first face is fresh and new.
You'll see each phase before we're through.

I see the moon. Can the moon see me?
Tell me, happy moon, what do you see?

My glow returns with slimmest crescent,
ever growing, effervescent.
Grinning as I orbit Earth,
I beam a smile at every birth.

I see the moon. Can the moon see me?
Tell me, half-moon, what do you see?

Although a half seems to appear,
you view a quarter of my sphere.
I cast my glitter on the ocean,
riding waves of soothing motion.

I see the moon. Can the moon see me?
Tell me, growing moon, what do you see?

When I wax, I gain a hump,
rounded gibbous, nice and plump.
Single lines of camel trains
cut paths across Mongolian plains.

I see the moon. Can the moon see me?
Tell me, round moon, what do you see?

When my face is full and bright,
I cover Earth with all my light.
My gleam on towers will enthrall
at the love-filled Taj Mahal.

I see the moon. Can the moon see me?
Tell me, shrinking moon, what do you see?

When I start the phase of waning,
I lose light instead of gaining.
Still I orbit in rotation,
passing oceans and each nation.

I see the moon. Can the moon see me?
Tell me, daylit moon, what do you see?

In daytime, I can show resilience
and appear with muted brilliance.
Boats from Greece set off on sails
and slice the sea with foamy trails.

I see the moon. Can the moon see me?
Tell me, crescent moon, what do you see?

I see a tower curved a trifle
based on plans by Gustave Eiffel.
Loving couples sway and dance
by moonlight while in Paris, France.

I can't see the moon, though it can see me.
Tell me, new moon, what did you see?

I've seen your world with all my faces
while illuminating places.
Every month, I can recall
where I've let my moonbeams fall.

I see the moon, and the moon sees me.
Please, friend moon, stay close to me.

*Through every phase, I'll share delight
and offer peace with each good night.
Then when you're sleeping, tucked in snug,
I'll wrap you in a moonlit hug.*

ABOUT THE MOON

Planet Earth and our moon are part of a solar system that orbits, or circles, around the sun. It takes about a year for the Earth to complete one lap around this fiery star. It takes about a month for the moon to orbit our planet, and it takes twenty-four hours for Earth to spin through the sunshine of daytime and the darkness that falls when our side of the planet turns away from the sun.

Just like with Earth, one half of the moon is always illuminated by the light of the sun. The surface of the moon acts like a giant mirror, and the moonlight we see on Earth is really sunlight reflecting off the lunar landscape. Sometimes, we can see the entire illuminated area of the moon. That's what we call a full moon. But, because the moon and Earth are always shifting their positions in relation to the sun, usually we're only able to see a portion of the sunlit moon. These movements account for the changing appearance of the moon.

GLOSSARY

Beam: Rays of light, particularly when we see them as individual bands of illumination, such as when we draw the sun having fingers of outstretched light. When people are especially happy and full of smiles, we say they are beaming, too.

Brilliance: A particularly strong kind of brightness. Sometimes we describe especially sunny days as being full of brilliance.

Earth: The third planet from the sun and our home. Our nearest planetary neighbors are Venus, the second planet, and Mars, the fourth.

Effervescent: A person or object that seems to overflow with life, energy, or brilliance.

Gustave Eiffel: (1832-1923) A famous French architectural engineer and designer. His specialty was works made with metals like iron and steel. In addition to creating important bridges and the tower in Paris that bears his name, he designed the framework that supports the outer shape of the Statue of Liberty.

Illuminating: When light shines on an object, it has been illuminated.

Moon: Objects that orbit around planets and other masses in a solar system. Some planets have many moons. Earth has only one.

Orb: A three-dimensional round shape, such as a basketball, or a planet.

Orbit: The path that a planet takes during its rotation around the sun. It takes about 365 days—or one year—for Earth to orbit the sun. Moons follow orbital paths when they circle a planet. It takes just over 27 days for our moon to orbit the Earth.

Resilience: To be strong, hardy, and tough, even in the face of difficult conditions.

Rotation: A pattern of movement where an object spins in a predictable and repetitive way, such as the way Earth spins through the sun's light each day.

Sphere: Just like an orb, a sphere is a three-dimensional round shape.

Sun: A star that serves as the center of our solar system with its pulsing energy and light. Eight planets orbit the sun, including Earth.

NEW MOON

The lunar cycle begins when sunlight
fully strikes the side of the moon
facing away from Earth, leaving the
rest of the surface darkened and
almost invisible from our planet.

WAXING CRESCENT

As the moon continues its lunar orbit,
its shifting orientation allows us to begin
to see sunlight reflecting off the surface
of the moon, and a slim, crescent-shaped
curve of light becomes visible from Earth.

FULL MOON

When the moon is halfway through the lunar cycle, it is
halfway through its rotation around the Earth. At this
point, its entire surface again faces the sun, but now the
Earth lies between the sun and the moon, so we can see
the full face of the moon reflecting sunlight.

WANING GIBBOUS

Lunar phases reverse their appearances while
the moon completes its orbiting journey around
Earth. The areas of the moon that brightened
at the beginning of the lunar cycle are the first
to darken, and we see less light as the visible
surface of the sunlit moon shrinks, or wanes.

THE LUNAR CYCLE

WAXING QUARTER

This sunlit exposure continues to wax, or increase, until half of the visible orb appears to shine, but really we are seeing only one-fourth, or a quarter, of the moon's round sphere.

WAXING GIBBOUS

In the ancient language of Latin, the word "gibbus" means "hump," and the gibbous moon appears to be growing a hump as more than half of its illuminated surface comes into view.

WANING QUARTER

The sunlit surface of the moon continues to fade from view until we can see only half of its illuminated face, or one quarter of the sphere.

WANING CRESCENT

As the moon moves back toward the position of fully facing the sun, our view of its sunlit surface shrinks to a lingering sliver of light.

NEW MOON

The lunar cycle is complete when the moon returns to the point where its illuminated surface fully faces the sun. At this point, the moon lies between Earth and the sun.

NOTE FROM THE AUTHOR

"I see the moon, and the moon sees me."

So began the folk lullaby that my mother sang to me as a child and that I sang to my young sons, years later. The comforting words of this tune helped to spark my lifelong affection for an ever-changing silvery orb.

While creating this text, I consulted with academic experts and reviewed online resources. I also drew from decades of my own casual observations of the moon. For many years, I lived with my family on a farm in southern Wisconsin, and we followed the evolving paths and phases of the moon during every lunar cycle and the changing seasons. A lifetime of travels inspired this text, too. I have visited many of the places illustrated in this book, and I still dream of seeing the rest.

"Hello, Mr. Moon," I often say out loud when I spot my old friend. Even though the appearance of this sphere shifts with its every rising, the moon remains my steadfast and reassuring companion wherever I am.

When my parents were courting in 1946, they lived in different parts of the United States. Sometimes, to feel a little closer, they sang to one another through the moon. When I see the moon and think about family members who are faraway, I do the same thing. It's just as the lullaby said:

"I see the moon, and the moon sees me.
The moon sees the one who I'd like to see.
God bless the moon, and god bless me,
And god bless the one who I'd like to see."

ACKNOWLEDGMENTS

Thanks to Britt Scharringhausen, associate professor and chair of physics and astronomy at Beloit College, and to Carl Mendelson, Beloit College emeritus professor of geology, for their expert review of the manuscript for this book.

For my parents, with love:
Henry S. Bausum (1924–2019)
and Dolores B. Bausum,
who sang to the moon, each other, and me
throughout 71 years of marriage
—AB

To my loving parents,
Dongjig Han and Jeesung Ahn
—KEH

ONLINE RESOURCES

Yearlong View of the Phases of the Moon
Hosted by the National Aeronautics and Space Administration (NASA).
https://moon.nasa.gov/resources/5/moon-phases-2017/

NASA Science—Solar System Exploration
Scientists at NASA explain and illustrate the workings of our solar system.
https://solarsystem.nasa.gov/

NASA Science—Earth's Moon
Available resources explain the phases of the moon, provide corrections of common
misunderstandings about it, explore the lunar surface, and more.
https://moon.nasa.gov/

Phases of the Moon
U.S. Naval Observatory illustrations of lunar phases.
https://aa.usno.navy.mil/faq/docs/moon_phases.php

What the Moon Looks Like Now
U.S. Naval Observatory real-time imagery.
https://aa.usno.navy.mil/imagery/moon

FOR FURTHER READING

Gibbons, Gail. *The Moon Book*. New York: Holiday House, 1997.
An introduction to moon science for children ages 4 to 8.

Johnson, Katherine. *Reaching for the Moon: The Autobiography of NASA Mathematician Katherine Johnson*. New York: Atheneum Books for Young Readers, 2019.
Presidential Medal of Freedom recipient Katherine Johnson recounts her work as a NASA mathematician in this autobiography for ages 10 and up.

Shetterly, Margot Lee with Winifred Conkling. Illustrated by Laura Freeman.
Hidden Figures: The True Story of Four Black Women and the Space Race. New York: HarperCollins, 2018.
The author behind the Hollywood film with this title shares the same story for children ages 4 to 8.

_____. *Hidden Figures Young Readers' Edition*. New York: HarperCollins, 2016.
This youth edition of the adult title is suitable for readers ages 8 to 12.

Simon, Seymour. *The Moon*. New York: Simon & Schuster Books for Young Readers, 2003 (revised edition).
A photo-illustrated guide to the moon for ages 7 to 11.

_____. *Destination: Moon*. New York: HarperCollins, 2019.
The story of the first landing on the moon in 1969 by Apollo 11, for ages 6 to 10.

Thimmesh, Catherine. *Team Moon: How 400,000 People Landed Apollo 11 on the Moon*.
New York: Houghton Mifflin Company, 2015.
The history behind the 1969 moon landing for children ages 10 to 12.